Find Fergus

by Elizabeth Dale and Becky Davies

FRANKLIN WATTS
LONDON•SYDNEY

Imran had come to stay with
Aunty Caroline.

He waved goodbye to his mum.

"We're going to have lots of fun,"
said Aunty Caroline.

Imran had brought Fergus,
his woolly rabbit, with him.
Aunty Caroline had knitted Fergus
for Imran when he was a baby.
He took Fergus everywhere.

Aunty Caroline and Imran went
into the garden.
"Shall we pick some blackberries?"
Aunty Caroline asked.
"Yes! Can we walk up Blackberry Hill?"
said Imran.

"Good idea," said Aunty Caroline.

It was a lovely sunny day.

As they walked up Blackberry Hill,

they saw butterflies flitting around

the flowers.

From the top of the hill, they could see

cows, sheep and horses.

Imran spotted a train in the distance.

It looked as small as a toy.

They picked some big, juicy blackberries.

"Come on," said Aunty Caroline.

"I'll race you home."

Off they ran, across the field.

Imran loved staying with Aunty Caroline.

When they got home, Imran and
Aunty Caroline made blackberry pie.
It was yummy!

At bedtime, Imran looked around
for Fergus.
"Aunty," he asked, "have you seen
Fergus? I can't find him."
"Maybe you dropped him
in the garden," said Aunty Caroline.
"Let's go and look."

Aunty Caroline and Imran looked
all around the garden,
but Fergus wasn't there.
"I must have dropped him
up on the hill," said Imran.
"We have to go and look for him!"
"We can't go now," said Aunty Caroline.
"It's too late."
"But I can't go to sleep without
him," Imran said with a frown.

Aunty Caroline shook her head.

"It will be too dark to find Fergus,"

she said.

"We'll look in the morning."

Imran turned to follow Aunty Caroline
into the house when he noticed
a long piece of white wool in
the rose bush. He picked it up.
"Look," he cried. "I think this wool is
from Fergus!"

Aunty Caroline shone her torch to see
where the trail of wool went.
"It looks as if Fergus got caught
on the bush and started
to come undone," she said.
"So the wool will lead us to him,"
cried Imran. "Come on!"

Imran and Aunty Caroline followed
the wool along the path back up the hill.

And there, at the top, was Fergus!

"Oh Fergus!" Imran cried, hugging him.

"Look at your poor leg!"

"At least you found him,"

said Aunty Caroline.

"Now home to bed."

In bed, Imran snuggled up to Fergus.
"I'll never ever lose him again,"
he told Aunty Caroline.

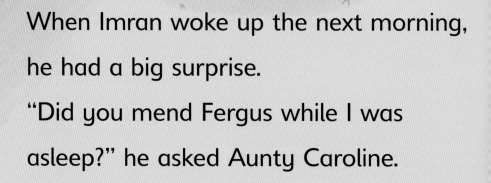

When Imran woke up the next morning,
he had a big surprise.

"Did you mend Fergus while I was
asleep?" he asked Aunty Caroline.

"Yes," she smiled.

"Oh, thank you," cried Imran,

cuddling Fergus.

"He's as good as new!"

Story order

Look at these 5 pictures and captions.
Put the pictures in the right order
to retell the story.

1

Imran could not find Fergus.

2

Imran went to stay with Aunty Caroline.

3

Imran found a trail of wool.

4

Imran took his toy rabbit Fergus out.

5

Imran found Fergus.

Guide for Independent Reading

This series is designed to provide an opportunity for your child to read on their own. These notes are written for you to help your child choose a book and to read it independently.

In school, your child's teacher will often be using reading books which have been banded to support the process of learning to read. Use the book band colour your child is reading in school to help you make a good choice. *Find Fergus* is a good choice for children reading at Turquoise Band in their classroom to read independently.

The aim of independent reading is to read this book with ease, so that your child enjoys the story and relates it to their own experiences.

About the book

When Imran stays with Aunty Caroline, he loses his favourite toy, a rabbit called Fergus. Luckily, Fergus has left a trail that Imran can follow to find him.

Before reading

Help your child to learn how to make good choices by asking:
"Why did you choose this book? Why do you think you will enjoy it?"
Look at the cover together and ask: "What do you think the story will be about?" Ask your child to think of what they already know about the story context. Then ask your child to read the title aloud.
Ask: "Who do you think Fergus is in the story?"
Remind your child that they can sound out a word in syllable chunks if they get stuck.
Decide together whether your child will read the story independently or read it aloud to you.

During reading

Remind your child of what they know and what they can do independently. If reading aloud, support your child if they hesitate or ask for help by telling the word. If reading to themselves, remind your child that they can come and ask for your help if stuck.

After reading

Support comprehension by asking your child to tell you about the story. Use the story order puzzle to encourage your child to retell the story in the right sequence, in their own words. The correct sequence can be found on the next page.

Help your child think about the messages in the book that go beyond the story and ask: "Why do you think Fergus is so important to Imran? Why do you think toys that have been made for you are extra special?" Give your child a chance to respond to the story: "Did you have a favourite part? Do you have a favourite toy or other item that is special to you?"

Extending learning

Help your child understand the story structure by using the same sentence patterning and adding different elements. "Let's make up a new story about Fergus. Where might he get lost this time and how could Imran find him again? How about in the supermarket or at the park?"

In the classroom, your child's teacher may be teaching about recognising punctuation marks. Ask your child to identify some question marks and exclamation marks in the story and then ask them to practise reading the whole sentences with appropriate expression.

Franklin Watts
First published in Great Britain in 2020
by The Watts Publishing Group

Series Editors: Jackie Hamley and Melanie Palmer
Series Advisors: Dr Sue Bodman and Glen Franklin
Series Designers: Peter Scoulding and Cathryn Gilbert

A CIP catalogue record for this book is
available from the British Library.

ISBN 978 1 4451 7158 6 (hbk)
ISBN 978 1 4451 7160 9 (pbk)
ISBN 978 1 4451 7161 6 (library ebook)

Printed in China

Franklin Watts
An imprint of
Hachette Children's Group
Part of The Watts Publishing Group
Carmelite House
50 Victoria Embankment
London EC4Y 0DZ

An Hachette UK Company
www.hachette.co.uk

www.reading-champion.co.uk

For Wilma,
who is one of the most
caring people I know.
– E.D.

Answer to Story order: 2, 4, 1, 3, 5